THE MAGIC HOUSE

story *by* Robyn Harbert Eversole

paintings by Peter Palagonia

ORCHARD BOOKS · NEW YORK

Orchard Books, 387 Park Avenue South, New York, NY 10016

Manufactured in the United States of America. Printed by General Offset Company, Inc. Bound by Horowitz/Rae. Book design by Mina Greenstein. The text of this book is set in 18 point ITC Novarese Medium. The illustrations were prepared on boards with wax base color leads and oil paints. 10 9 8 7 6 5 4 3 2 1

Library of Congress Cataloging-in-Publication Data
Eversole, Robyn Harbert. The magic house / story by Robyn Harbert Eversole ; paintings by Peter Palagonia.   p.   cm. "A Richard Jackson book"—Half t.p.
Summary: April, who sees her house in an imaginative way that can turn the stairs into a waterfall and the living room into a desert, tries to share her vision with her older sister Meredith as Meredith practices her ballet steps.
ISBN 0-531-05924-3.   ISBN 0-531-08524-4 (lib. bdg.)
|1. Imagination—Fiction.   2. Sisters—Fiction.   3. Ballet dancing—Fiction.| I. Palagonia, Peter, ill.   II. Title.   PZ7.E9235Mag   1992
|E|—dc20   91-17824

To Chip Eversole—
brother and wonderkid
—R.H.E.

For Ben and Barbara
—P.P.

The house at 519 Kipperney Street belonged to April. Her mother and her father and her older sister Meredith lived there too, but the house was April's, and the house was magic.

In the middle of the house was a waterfall. It ran from the second floor to the first. April could slide down it and never get wet.

On the first floor was a desert. The ground was yellow and everywhere there were big cactuses. April could climb on the cactuses and they would never prickle her.

Down in the basement was a cave. Two monsters lived there, way back in the corner. They muttered and growled when April's mother fed them baskets of clothes.

The monsters weren't very scary, but they were monsters nonetheless, and April was proud to have them in her magic house.

The only trouble with the house at 519 Kipperney Street was April's older sister Meredith. Meredith didn't believe the house was magic. When she walked by, the waterfall stopped being a waterfall. "Don't slide down the stairs," Meredith would say.

When April was in the desert and Meredith came along,
the desert became a living room.
"Stop climbing on the furniture," Meredith would say,
as she sat down to practice the piano. Loudly.

"When you're older, you'll do lots of things," Meredith told
April one day. "You'll learn piano, and ballet. Like me."
Meredith held on to the kitchen counter and lifted one leg
in the air.

April lifted one leg in the air without holding on to the counter. "I do lots of things already," she said.

"I'm going to be a
swan in the recital,"
said Meredith.
"Will you get to
dance in water?"
April asked.
"Not real water, no,"
Meredith said. She
was having trouble
with one of her steps
and frowned at April.
"We're supposed to
pretend."

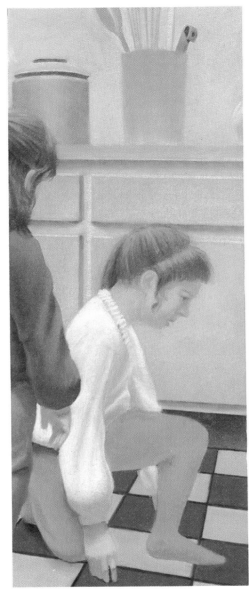

Meredith did a leap in the middle of the kitchen, and the pots
and pans in the cupboards shook.
"Swans don't THUMP," she said, and frowned again.

But April knew something Meredith didn't.
April knew that, for weeks and weeks, water had been
    tumbling down
        the waterfall
            and making a beautiful blue lake at the bottom.

"I don't feel like a swan," Meredith said. "I don't look like a swan.
I'm a dancer *THUMP*ing in the middle of the kitchen."
The pots and pans shook again.

"Come with me," April said. . . .

April took Meredith to the front hall, right to the edge of the beautiful blue lake. "This is a lake," she told Meredith. "A beautiful blue lake with reeds all around and swans in the middle."

"Oh, April," Meredith said. "Don't act dumb. This is the front hall."

April sat down on
the stairs, which were
just stairs and not
a waterfall.
"Practice here
anyway," she said.

Meredith did a few more leaps, thumping a little less
with each one, sailing and soaring more and more like a swan.

Reeds sprouted along the walls.

April felt water running past
her hands. It lapped across the floor,
reflecting Meredith.

And when Meredith lifted her arms at her sides, April saw wings.

"Do you see the lake?" April asked Meredith. "Do you see it?"
Meredith didn't say anything. She was gliding over the water . . .
and the next moment

she wasn't Meredith at all, but a white swan
on the beautiful blue lake in the middle of April's magic house.

"Do you see the lake?" April asked again

and she knew—no matter what Meredith said later—

that the answer at that moment was:

"Yes."